ROAD

A postlapsarian Comedy

BY

JOSIAH MORGAN

D1178733

FERAL DOVE BOOKS
SEATTLE
2022

PART

ONE

"Your teeth! They're yours?"

—Bill Heath

There's a crash and the microwave is gone.
Here it begins, the rest of the world.

It begins with the realisation that nobody is listening. The rest of the world, through the microwave-shaped hole in the window. They had been sitting there, the three of them cosy on the leather couch, some multi-limbed monolith, each head scrolling through instant photos on whatever latest device, and then the crash and now they're up on their feet, single-cell naturals, looking out from this place, knowing it's all got to change now, it's all going to change because the microwave was inside before and it's outside now. Barni threw it. Nearly without thinking. The rest of it begins without thinking when nobody is listening to what Barni wants to say.

Barni watches the hands of his friends transform into claws. They're shrieking at him words that don't make sense, that's, you've fucked, that's it, we thought you were over, everything, all this, fucked up, stuff, we thought it was fine, we thought we were just becoming friends again, you've, fuck, we thought you knew what you were doing, you told us you were seeing a shrink, you told us, you told us, you've fucked it Barni, everything, all of, it, it's fucked. The claws are tearing at his clothing.

For a brief moment, Barni thinks he sees the world the way it really is: impossible to replicate in words.

They kick him out of the house, them and their talons, they kick him out with nothing, they take everything from him, they even take the hole in the window. That was something that should have belonged to Barni.
And that's it, he's out in the world, family-less, bleeding from a little hole on the side of his neck (God knows how that got there) on his thirtieth birthday, bursting with energy because he wants to tell anyone that will listen that he just heard the voice of God.
"Yeah, so?" says the lady behind the counter. "God's everywhere these days, order's up."

So now there's a hot meal in Barni's stomach, but all the money's gone. What's left is the rest of the world, but before that, the road.

He flickers in and out of consciousness past the roadkill. Somebody calls out to him for spare change, that's how he knows he's not all gone just yet. Tell it again, he says to himself, Tell it again.

I was in the bathroom. I was shaving against the grain. I heard a knock on my window. It wasn't a knock. She was a pigeon pecking her beak. How do I know it was a her? He was a pigeon pecking his beak. Against the window. Not sure what it was that compelled me to, but I opened it, let the pigeon in. He came and sat on the third, no, fourth tile from the toilet, did a little shit, perched himself on the shower rail, started speaking. "Hey." He said. "I'm God." He said. "Fuck off." I said. "Am I hallucinating right now?" I said. "Did somebody slip something into my coffee? Is this some sick joke?" "No. You're not hallucinating right now. And nobody slipped anything into your coffee. I'm God, and this is what I look like. Best get used to it." He said. "What the fuck are you doing here, talking to me?" I said. "Oh, no reason. Just felt like saying hello." And just like that the pigeon was gone again (in absentia) and I rushed downstairs to tell everybody and none of them were having it and I just, I got so frustrated that I, I just, threw it, I threw it out the window. My leftovers were still in it.

He tells this to himself as he walks the state highway, not even bothering to stick his thumb up. Barni has no idea where he's going, not really, he's just moving because his feet tell him he has to, no rest for the wicked, a cliché, huh, no matter, that is, he's moving, he is, until he stops, all of a sudden, after a few hours, when he hears the sound of pigeons in the distance.

The song of the bird paralyses Barni for a second. He finds himself unable to move toward the noise but afraid to move backward. He's afraid of what the pigeons might prove. If he stays where he is, he can imagine the possibilities forever, wonder what God wanted to tell him, wonder why birds. If he moves backward, well, he can't do that, the road behind seeming to vanish suddenly, going back a literal, material impossibility. But if he moves forward, what then? What then? He arrives to see nothing at all, the pigeon imaginary, conjured in his head. Or he arrives and once again it's God, leading him forward, telling him nothing but laying the future down in splints and disarray. Or, God forbid, worst of all, he arrives and the pigeon is there, but that's all it is, a pigeon, sitting in a tree, a false signifier during something that hasn't even begun yet. No, best to stay put, camp out here. He takes his jacket, lays it out underneath his prostrate body, it's a cold night, but whatever, he won't sleep if it's just his body on this hard surface, anyway, so he sleeps in a t-shirt and jeans, shivering, his holy left-sock probably worth taking off, but where would he put it?

Never mind. Sleep does not come easily out here. Every time Barni drifts off, he's startled awake again by the sirens of a cop car or the headlights of an interstate bus. Eventually he gives up on losing consciousness, drifts between images of himself as a child and the noise of cicadas, geez, it's that time already, and just like this the days fade one into another until eventually some trucker notices Barni lying on the side of the road, stops to offer him some food, throws a few dollars at his feet, says "come on, the world don't stop here" and then keeps on driving. That's enough for Barni, "come on, the world don't stop here," enough to get him off the ground, to keep moving, toward the pigeons or toward no pigeons or toward something inside his own head, anything whatever. Barni's a sick animal in the endless granite desert, waiting to drink from that ornithological oasis.

Barni thinks for a second that the pigeon is asking him "what? what?" very fast, over and over, but as he gets closer he realises it's just this generic birdy braying.

It'd be disappointing if it weren't for the spectacle. Because Barni realises not a moment too soon that he's come across not just one pigeon but one massive barnyard full of them. GRUMPY'S PIGEON FARM, shouts the sign on the road-facing billboard in crumbling capital letters. The fence is bent, as if straining to hold the weight of the world around it, and what else is Barni going to do but step inside to have a look around, so look around he does. The pigeons don't offer too much, really – these ones don't say hello or play around – but there's a pantry in the corner and a tramping bag somebody's left next to an unclean litter-box (God knows why the cat is allowed in here, how many pigeons are lost to that other, elegant creature), so naturally Barni takes the stuff. Some cans of beans, some chickpeas, a bottle of lighter fluid, a half-used pen, some condoms (God knows how old), an unopened envelope addressed to Marjorie. And of course half a swig of whisky, which he gulps down on the spot. Best keep moving, not much else to look at. Turns out the sounds weren't a sign of divinity at all, just encouragement to keep going. But to keep going to what? To what?

That's when Barni hears a strange crashing noise above his head, feels burning heat from above, is half-blinded in the glare of a spotlight that resembles a Hollywood LED. Before he knows it he's strapped on a gurney, naked, unshaven pubes and all, and standing above him is a very tall person with the head of a bird. "Hey. Good to see you again." The bird unzips his fly and pulls out something that's almost a penis. He doesn't do anything with it, but it's just at Barni's eye level and honestly just a little unsettling. "I see you haven't been up to too much. That's a shame, Barni. You have potential. Real potential." A pause, quite a long one.

"Suck me off." And Barni does, but the bird's appendage doesn't seem to respond, at least not in recognisable terms. The pigeon yelps out laughter but all Barni hears is birdsong. "God, Barni, I wasn't serious, who do you think I am?" The bird says. "Didn't you know I hate faggots?"

The bird says. "Didn't you read my book in Sunday School as a kid?" The bird says. "What the fuck is this?" Barni says. "Am I dreaming?" Barni says. "No." Replies the bird. "But you might as well be. Get to work."

And just like that Barni's awake, sprawled on the floor of the barnyard, all the birds are gone, but the tramping pack's still there, complete with beans, chickpeas, lighter fluid, half-used pen, condoms, letter addressed to Marjorie. His underwear is a little sticky on the inside and he doesn't really know how to respond to that, and then the blinding headache hits and he's out cold, conscious and awake, but out cold, on the floor of a barn in the middle of nowhere, on a road to somewhere, a road to God knows where.

It takes four days before he's actually up and moving again. Even then, he only moves far enough to find a public cooking facility. These abound now, multiply, in the dilapidated ruins of what was once public enterprise. Not that Barni knows that.

It's twenty-six days after the barnyard incident when Barni finally plucks up the courage to open the sealed envelope addressed to Marjorie:

"Baby,

I am alone and when I am alone I regret thin[g]

In my dream last night, you told me off for gettin[g] too close to you. Can't handle all of this. Or any of the things you've told people I've done.

I keep looking in the mirror and feeling sick or feeling sick and then looking in the mirror to try and steady myself but it doesn't work. I can't help thinking about all the things I've done to you and I've started to regret more and more of them over time, you have to believe me.

I might be dead when you get this. Look after yourself. It wasn't you that did this, it was me. I've done my research.

One must imagine Sisyphus happy."

And there's now a whole new flurry of questions for Barni, like, the most basic one is that it's a suicide letter right? But Barni can't be sure of that, not quite, and anyway if the envelope stayed sealed then Marjorie never opened it, right? And why did the writer put it on a shelf in a dilapidated barnyard in the middle of nowhere? A barnyard that may or may not have been a pigeon farm at some point or another? Okay, so what's the point? The writer wrote all this down, Camus quote and all, and then, what, just upped and left? Said sayonara 'til the next life? A sudden gleaming pain in his lower intestine makes him keel over, need to shit, doesn't seem to be any facilities around, and then it happens, mess everywhere, Barni in his own stink, and just like that there's a bird (believe me!) bathing in the pools of it that have formed at the bottom of each trouser leg. "Really, Barni, you've got to learn to control these things." The bird says. "But, well, God has a way of paying back our dues." The bird says. "But I thought you were God." Barni says. "Oh, I am. I guess I have a way of paying back your dues." He says. "What fucking dues did I owe?" Asks Barni incredulously. "Well, come on." Says the bird. "You just read a letter addressed to somebody else, a suicide letter, no less. Diarrhoea was, I think, a bit of a low-end punishment, don't you?"

Barni doesn't know what to say to that, just lets out a string of noises, something like "buh-awuhhh-hmm-engggggg-kkkkkkkk-buh-buh-buh" and shakes his head at the same time.

God talks uninhibited for the first time.

"Really, though, Barni, you should have seen this coming. You should know better than anybody, really. Privacy barely exists anymore. I would have thought that your anonymity or your inscrutable lack of selfhood would have helped you understand the pure, heavy, sickening weight of what you were doing. Trampling on somebody else's business. I mean, really, Barni. But you've done it now. You've done it now. I'd hoped you'd only take the tramping pack. I have an important job for you to do. But never mind. Diarrhoea was a low-end punishment, but you've signed yourself up for a thankless job now.

Get yourself clean, I mean seriously, what the fuck, Barni?, and then find Marjorie. She won't come easy. Give her the letter. Tell her you read it. Then leave. It'll be unfulfilling, don't you worry. This is your purpose now. You impinged on knowledge that should have been kept secret for somebody else, and now you must bear the weight of that knowledge. Roll it up the hill." (A birdlike laugh). "You may as well think of yourself as an object, now, something belonging to me. I mean, really, Barni, free will?

You will find yourself echoing both Sisyphus and Eve. You ate the apple I delicately laid for you. Now you must roll the apple up the eternal hill." (A laugh). "I'm only joking of course. There are no rules. I'm just doing this because I feel like it."

And just like that, the bird's gone, it's just Barni, mythic hero, in his own shit on the road; bag, beans, chickpeas, pen, fluid; that heavy letter addressed to Marjorie.

Here is the shower head, and here is Barni, having what those in the biz call a Personal Existential Crisis (PEC, which, when said aloud, is pronounced like 'peck' by the initiated speaker). I mean, the water's not even running and underneath it is this big flunky slice of a man with his watershed eyes and asymmetric balance. And the man thinks he's just seen God, and he's got nowhere to go, and it cost him nothing to get into this shower, sure, but then it cost a couple of bucks to get the water going hot, and Barni wasn't about to take a cold shower, not in winter, okay, so he's just been sitting out on the street begging for spare change for a while, a scary man, smelly, covered in his own dried excrement, it took hours, you'd be surprised, but anyway, here's Barni, in the middle of his PEC about to put some dollars in the meter and turn the water on to hot.

When Barni was a kid, his parents had a shower enclosed in its own little vacuum. You'd shut the doors behind you and then it was just you and white walls, glistening with little specks of black mould. Okay, so it wasn't ideal, but it was somewhere to be alone, and somewhere that Barni came to do his thinking. He'd stood in that shower without water running plenty of times, most notably when Jenny told him age twelve that no, she wouldn't go out with him, actually, leave me alone, creep, and then threw the drawing he'd done for her in the green rubbish bin at the edge of the tennis court they had both been standing on. Barni hadn't played tennis too much after that, which had made him a little sad years later when he read the first section or two of Infinite Jest, actually, the tennis had been the reason he'd stopped, and he'd spent some time sitting in the shower after quitting that book, too, feeling like a failure once again.

The opening of a small wormhole, then. Barni, age twelve, rejected by Jenny. Barni, age nineteen, rejecting David Foster Wallace for the first time. Barni now, thirty, full-on PEC underway, about to scrub away something that literally came from inside himself.

Time travel is real in memory, and Barni is doing it.

He puts one toe into each hole in the drain grille and turns on the water. When Barni was a kid, it's hard to remember what age now, he'd read some instruction manual (obviously a joke) for a Do-It-Yourself (DIY) swimming pool. Plug the grille, water on, let it rise, water off, swim around, unplug grille, water drain, back to an empty shower and nobody knows you broke the rules. Barni never asked why the book didn't just suggest taking a bath. But, whatever, it didn't work anyway, Barni's toes didn't plug enough and there was too much empty space around the sides.

Well, really, it's worth knowing, probably, that if you were to see Barni walking along the street, you'd be much more likely to notice the empty space around him than Barni himself. Sure, you'd know a man was there, but you wouldn't look at him. The world around him would take on a slightly brighter hue. You might notice a misspelled corporate logo that you hadn't before. You might finally appreciate the color hot pink for the first time. Barni has this effect and he has this effect without even realizing it.

(Those units that kicked Barni out after the microwave incident have receded into dullness themselves without Barni around).

So: the water's running and Barni's feet are over the grille. Of course, he's not going to succeed at creating a homemade swimming pool, and even if he did, it wouldn't be homemade, it'd be Made In Public (MIP), a DIY MIP swimming pool, but anyway, the DIY MIP dream is exactly that, a dream. Instead, the only effect Barni's feet over the grille have is that his own dried diarrhoea doesn't come off, it just dampens and bits of it start floating around in the bottom of the water. It's probably not good for Barni's foot fungus, but then, what is, and actually, it takes Barni a surprisingly long time to recognize how disgusting the situation is, in fact, by then the water's running cold and Barni's quest for spare change wasn't worth anything after all.

A few dollars spent on a few minutes of hot water.
A worthwhile spending decision, wasted.

The shower head's spitting cold water angrily at Barni's head and he just has to get on with the cleansing job underway, so, fine, he does it with his bare hands and then rinses his hands off too. There's no real shower soap around, but what do you expect, it's a public shower, although in the next room over (concrete, of course) there's a public toilet with hand-soap, which will have to do. Barni leaves the shower running and makes a mad dash for the hand-soap, well and truly in the nude, which luckily nobody sees.

Spilling half of the soap he's collected on the way back to the shower is a crying shame, but Barni has no desire to extend this ordeal any longer, so he makes do with what he has, gets back under the water, gives himself a quick rinse, this time with a fragrance resembling something nice in the palm of his hand, and then stands there in the nude for an hour or so to drip dry. He doesn't have a towel, of course.

While he's in there drying, he thinks about a few things and notices a few others.

He thinks about:

^my mother saying 'I want you to drink your milk, I want you to drink your milk.'

losing my virginity to Maya Richter in the women's bathroom at high school.

Humphrey Bogart in Casablanca.

the way Gillian Anderson looks so beautiful and so afraid in The X Files.

the couch in my father's living room was so uncomfortable because the cushions jutted out too far.

the elderly woman at my father's funeral who complimented the sandwiches at the reception.

how terrible it _would be to die drowning.

the fact that maybe I should try to get some sleep soon, good sleep.

the fact that there's no good reason for me
                                        to actually try to find this Marjorie
anyway.

the fact that there's no good reason for me not to.

                                                                    '

my mother saying 'I want you to drink your milk. I want you to drink your milk

He notices:

the mould on the roof is a funny constellation and looks a little bit like a rabbit trying to chase a zebra, but then he looks at it for a little too long and the zebra transforms into a man with three legs limping along trying to get away from an alligator, and the alligator is much bigger than the man so he's definitely going to be eaten soon, but in this glorious pre-death moment he's still fighting, this man with three legs, he's still fighting, and it's there cemented on the ceiling in a patch of mould, a crystalline moment of terror in a public shower, it would stay there forever if only the mould would stop growing. If only the mould wasn't alive. A living organism creating an accidental portrait of death.

above the towel rail (of which, of course, there's no towel) on the windowsill is a key. God knows what it could be used for – there aren't any locks around – but Barni takes it anyway. He isn't taking any chances.

He's alone, shitless, with a key, some beans, some chickpeas, lighter fluid, a half-used pen, and that unsealed letter addressed to Marjorie, that's Barni, with all these items, they're stored in a bag, a tramping bag that's getting heavier one tiny item at a time.

3

The Man Outside The Shop (The MOTS) is sick of being surrounded by this much language.

"board recognizes cultural responsibility to the indigenous population. That's what the document says, and we have to act on it with our policies about" … "long black for MIKE that's a LONG BLACK for Mike" … "only need half as much iron as women and vegetarian women actually need half more than" … "missed that, could you repeat" … "Mike? MIKE?" … "anonymously get in touch about the" … "help you?" "short black for EZRA hey there you go have a great" … "I, I answered to, I was" … "Mike!" … "finish your lunch before I buy you the" … "Mike?" … "coffee up! coffee" … "yes so take IBPS, the RPB and PO versions, yes, both of them, and then move on to SBI PO and JPSC and then plug that into the FPI system so you" … "Mike" … "go home" … "latte for FELICITY latte for FELICITY" … "MIKE" … "ating my tools" … "fridge in the garage might have something similar in" … "absolutely fucked, had a tacky on the side of the road. Somehow I spent a few hundred bucks in a couple of" … "care what you think" … and so on … endlessly … and so on …

The Mots is new around these parts. His blanket made the journey over the State line with him, developing a chronic case of holiness along the way. As did a sign, HOMELESS / ANY MONEY WANTED / FOOD AND SMOKES / GOD BLESS. A woman in high heels click-clacks past him, which is distracting, if only for a moment. His eyes search her legs for an indication of imperfection. He can't find it. Either his eyesight's as perfect as her legs, or they're both in the midst of affection by unrecognized physical defects. The street he's perched on is long and irremovably public. It's a whole new world for The Mots, after this journey from place to place was forced upon him by the gradual horror of being an alive person in the previous town.

At first, in the last place, things had been okay. There was only a small amount of foot traffic, but you still made money if you chose to sit at one of three profit-turning corners. The one outside the pub. The one outside the post office. The one outside the grocery store.

The roads were quiet, and the lack of a large population had meant there were plenty of places to sleep uninterrupted.

The two local police officers, Bobby Joe and Connie 'Carcass' Black had to put on a tough front and ask The Mots and the other homeless folk around town to move on from reputable places like the public park or the bridge that attached the local school to the woods, but otherwise, The Mots and folk like him could settle down wherever they wanted, get a good eight hours of sleep. Moving daily with the slow pace of the calendar and no bills to pay. Until all of a sudden little Jimmy Shue was found dead face-down in his bowl of cereal.

The coroner said that little Jimmy Shue had been poisoned by lead and in a town where everybody knows everybody that didn't go down so well. Jimmy's dad was a pencil manufacturer at a factory just outside the limits of the town. The Shue parents were taken into custody almost immediately. This served two purposes. For one thing, they were prime suspects. For another, custody kept them safe from the community, who turned rabid, feral, talons emerging from their knuckles. The Shue parents lost everything including the spaces they used to inhabit. Police officers would walk past the holding rooms and forget they were even there. The Shue parents overheard numerous conversations that would convict a police officer in a second, but they forgot as readily as they listened. They forgot everything except their dead son.

The Shue household became a Temporary Autonomous Zone. It was graffitied by local teens with slurs like CHILD-KILLERS and PEDOS (the coroner found no evidence of sexual assault). On one particularly humid afternoon, one of the local housewives, Amanda Hardwicke, stepped out of her house across the street and threw a rock through what was once little Jimmy Shue's bedroom window. She was taking the anger she felt toward her husband out on the Shue property. She felt justified because here, in this place, Shue had become a synonym for Killer, Shue had become a synonym for Enemy, Shue had come to mean Whatever The Town Wanted It To Mean. The town vagrants moved in, every single one except The Mots, who preferred the rough peace of the outdoors. Normalcy returned and the town re-engaged its typical slowness.

A month later, when it was both clear that there was no evidence to convict and that it was safe enough for the Shue parents to return home, the vagrants were found dead. Poisoned.

The coroner had no clue.
The Shue parents had no clue.
The town was in uproar.
The Mots was blamed.
(The Mots was not to blame).
The Mots fled the town.
Everybody calmed down.
The Shue parents were found dead a week later.

And here he is, The Mots, on a street corner in a busy city, living a life entirely unlike before. All activities the same – bumming, begging, rough sleeping – sure, but the fabric of the universe a little altered, more hostile.

Back in that small town, everybody is still in uproar. The coroner is in distress. Everybody is unsure who to blame, every single one a hypochondriac. Along a back road (not too far from town) there's a broken piece of plumbing (not too far from GRUMPY'S PIGEON FARM). The pipe spurts lead nitrate like a poisoned phallus, spurts it in such a way that it connects directly with the Shue water supply and only the Shue water supply. The poor kid died of lead nitrate poisoning, the poor vagrants, the poor parents.

In that small town lodged between the road taken by The Mots and the road taken by that familiar everyman Barni, the people died because of water, nitrate, and lead. Lead. That name afforded to the round black hole in the centre of any pencil. The invisible substance that killed little Jimmy Shue. A tool that's both the pen and the sword.

The sword is mightier than the pen. Heed it.

He's been walking for days since the shower with very little rest so it's no wonder that when Barni sees skyscrapers in the distance, a small sliver of relief escapes his body in a yelp that sounds not unlike a small dog. It's remarkable, really, that he's excited to see something signifying so many people – not like Barni, not the way he used to be, anyway. At age twelve (only a week before the Jenny thing, come to think of it, they could have been connected somehow), which is a little too old for things like this to happen, Barni had been unable to work out the locking mechanism on the public Port-A-Potty and it had been a whole ordeal with school staff trying to get him out and heaps of kids gathered around laughing, jeering, eating cheapo candy from the school café. That was just one incident of many that had Barni wishing that really he'd just Left Himself Alone to Work This Out; he hadn't been happy to see people then.

He had been happy to see people at his father's funeral. Not that he had wanted to talk to them. But it had felt good to see, really see, that his father had mattered. The apple doesn't fall far from the tree, Barni thought, in an attempt to boost his own spirits. It felt good to see that his father had mattered to this many people, and the apple doesn't fall far from the tree. And then the woman who had introduced herself as Taisia complimented the bland funereal sandwiches and then promptly walked out, four sandwiches in her left hand, a walking puff of eau de toilette. The apple doesn't fall far from the tree, and my father is dead. So, anyway, whatever, Barni's glad to see a place with lots of people again and a little surprised that he feels this way, but it's still, he thinks, a good six hours walk to the skyscrapers (Barni isn't the type to hitch-hike, oh no), so he chooses to set up camp behind a road sign and hopes the cops don't come past.

The road sign is planted at a fork in the road signalling that the first path (the one Barni just came from and will continue on) is STATE HIGHWAY 7: TO CIVIL-ISATION. Yeah, that's exactly what the sign says. Wait, what the fuck? Anyway, the rest of the sign is pretty straightforward, quietly indicating that the other path (the one Barni's unfamiliar with) leads directly to some place called FORDYCE (has a bit of a ring of myth to it) forty-three kilometres away.

And he's lying down behind the road sign, skipping dinner tonight. He's been dumpster diving along the way, eaten a surprising amount of perfectly good fresh produce because of it, even if it has been at infrequent times. Sure, he's got those chickpeas, those beans, but Barni's never been big on legumes anyway, and he has this weird gut feeling that they're going to come in handy someday, you never know when you might be stuck on a path with no dumpsters around, it's hard to say.

.

Barni's taking care of the future for once in his life

It's with possibility in hand that serendipity delivers Barni to the same street corner The Mots is sitting on.

They nearly miss each other, actually, because The Mots is half asleep in this waking-dreaming state, listening to everything (all that language) go past but in the midst of some unconscious encounter with the id. The visuals The Mots are seeing are increasingly complex, a set of Matryoshka Doll-like mosaics, all nested inside each other. Faces inside eyes, faces inside eyes. Teeth made up of faces. Faces made up of teeth. The Mots isn't on anything, this is just how his brain works, besides, it's been ages since there's been much else to keep him preoccupied. So, in his head, everything shrinks down to size. The world is made up of a collation of smaller things. He's dreaming this compartmentalized universe up when he's woken by the sound of something metal clanging on the concrete.

He shudders at the sight of what must be somebody's housekey, figures he might as well return it to its rightful owner. Talking isn't The Mots' strong suit; he barks out the phrase "key" which causes somebody to turn around on his heel. The first impression The Mots gets is that this guy, despite his age, seems to move just like a kid. That prompts a strange stirring. Some kind of classist fear. This boy-like man seems, to The Mots, like just another rich-hiker (Rich-hiker's the name The Mots gives to the young folk with money who dramatically exit their home city one day with nothing on their back but a bag of clothes and some canned food, but secretly make their hitch-hiking trip with thousands of dollars sitting in their bank accounts.

It's a staged depravity, this rich-hiking is, a performance of class solidarity, a way of re-integrating into the upper-class elite with the sensation of having been in poverty once but ascended past it. An affirmation of the fact that hard work wins the day, and anybody can go from rags to riches. A clever myth constructed by those who don't know about those who do). But Barni's not just another rich-hiker, something The Mots understands the moment Barni barks back, "not mine. Keep it," which The Mots does.

Here they are, the intentional vagrant, the incidental vagrant, standing at the edge of a temporal cliff-face, some of the world behind them, the rest of it in front of them. Here they are, looking at each other, barely thinking a thought in the world. There's not much to do. So Barni sits. And stares. Outcasts at the edge of something big, that would be experienced in small bits and pieces. A meal cut up with a knife and fork. Easy to swallow.

For the first time in a long time, pigeons don't cross Barni's mind, not even for a second.

Sitting and staring, he thinks of nothing much at all.

They become comrades of the street for a while, learning small details about each other every day. It takes a while – a few weeks – for The Mots to open up about the deaths in that small town that forced this venture upon him, and even then Barni doesn't get the full story. "Come from Fordyce." Says The Mots. "Bunch of people died there. My friends. Some of them. Cops thought it was me. Wasn't. Came here." Says The Mots. Barni doesn't really know how to respond, honestly he barely understands anything The Mots has just said, so he just stands up and proclaims "well, it's good to be here with you," is what Barni proclaims, and it probably is good, better than being stuck between places, people and things.

It's after that conversation that Barni starts to understand the skittishness of The Mots. They'll be walking together toward no place in particular and The Mots will suddenly halt, look around, hide behind or under whatever nearest monolith. The Mots is a classic paranoiac, actually, but he doesn't seem to realise this about himself. Instead, it's Barni who broaches the subject, suggests to The Mots that he might be a little too, "mmm, paranoid, like a hypochondriac but about nothing much in particular," that's the indelicate phraseology Barni spits out across a table in a shelter for other unfortunates and uncommon types. The Mots garbles out something that might be an accusation in response. "What you doing here? Huh? Why you come here? You looking for me?"

But after sleeping on it The Mots is back to normal and pretty easily comprehends that Barni's just another dirty cowboy trying to do what he can to keep on keeping on.

Still, Barni has to do all the shopping. The Mots says that the folks behind the counter in the supermarket might be up to something. He doesn't want to find himself anywhere there might be a camera (this bit is getting increasingly hard as time goes on and the world seems to want to record everything, even the things nobody will ever have the time to watch back) because he doesn't want his face recognised. Recognised by who, he doesn't seem to have an answer to, but, oh, just anyone, and fair enough, who can blame him. Accused of murder once, on the run for the rest of his life from nothing in particular.

Running for the sake of it.

Time passes and it's getting harder and harder for the homeless to fend for money. Cash has forever complemented this near-feudal social system of the underclass, but that's starting to change now. More and more people are paying for things with chipped cards, phones, watches, whatever's most portable, and more and more the homeless aren't paying for things at all, just hoping for the charity of whoever happens to be moving by at any one specific time. Money has never quite, hmm, 'trickled' down here, but it's certainly tinkled down, coinage dropped accidentally or intentionally, clanging against the concrete paving stones, the harmonious music of some kind of fiction that keeps us living.

Stories dropped from the pockets of the better-off.

Walking down the main street in-between the closing-in skyscrapers there are the mega-rich and the faux-rich entering the Gucci stores, the Prada stores. Their pockets are secure, their finances tight, locked behind a four-digit number and a microchip. Around seven in the morning, just before opening time, it's possible to witness the well-suited security guards uprooting the city muck who've been sleeping out all night on the concrete beside all that air-conditioned empty space. One could sleep among all that fabric and all those other elemental riches. And yet it remains: the empty space.

Barni's leaving The Mots to shop for food with the small bits of loose change they've collected in the last couple of days. They've got enough for some bread and fruit at the very least, and beyond that Barni might be able to squeeze some extra purchases in if he's clever about it.

That's when he hears a humanoid voice from the gutter to his left which well and truly steals his attention.

"Eyy-you. Can you-wellp me." Says the humanoid voice, which belongs to some poor man who looks shockingly similar to an armadillo.

To which Barni says, "uh, uh….., sure…., I guess."

The armadillo man turns toward the gutter grille next to him and shoves his hand down inside it. He somehow produces not one or two but eleven cans of wet dog food and sets them up as a tower in front of himself. All of a sudden the man's standing up and he's actually somehow shockingly handsome, looks kind of like a normal human being, if a little off-kilter. He grabs Barni's fore-arm, kicks him in the gut and removes Barni's tramping bag.

Barni has no idea what the fuck is happening, so he's kind of flailing his limbs out around him like a soggy towel, it's all very ineffective, the now-handsome ex-armadillo is making a real fool of Barni, he's tipped the tramping bag upside down and rifling through it but doesn't show too much interest in any of the non-consumable items, definitely doesn't make anything of that crucial letter. He takes the can of beans, the can of chickpeas, sets them safely aside underneath the gutter grille whilst Barni rolls around clutching his stomach a few feet away. He empties Barni's pockets of the grovelled coins, too, hides those underneath the grille, and then sits back down, a dirty inhuman creature again.

It takes Barni a few minutes to recover, at which point he stands up and makes a dash for his stuff: the money, the food. That crumpled-up other being just shouts "no!" and that's enough to make Barni stop what he's doing for some reason. The strange origami animal passes on some advice: "take a break. Everyone around these parts seems to know who you are now, Barni. That friend of yours, he's got connections. He's a worthwhile one to have on your side. So take a break. Stop grovelling. You'll be well-fed as long as you're on good terms with him. Trust me. You'll be in luck tonight."

Barni just nods his head, what else can he do?

"Me, though, ha, me, well, he doesn't like me too much. Things like this, I guess. I hurt his friends too much. Or his friends tell many stories about me too much. Still, you tell him you had a run in with Small Gordie and you'll find the heavens open up above you. He'll take pity on you, he will. I been eating these cans of dog food for the last two months of my life. I say no, no, no more. So I take your cans, your beans, your chickpeas. I take your cans of food so you take my dog food in exchange. A fair exchange, hmm? You tell the old man that I paid my way. I paid my way."

He stops talking and just at that moment right in front of Barni's eyes Small Gordie seems to shrink; a contracting elastic band. He shrinks so much so that he flattens into something almost two dimensional, Barni has to blink and blink again to make sure his eyes aren't playing up, and then Gordie's gone, slipped down the drain, taken Barni's dollars and Barni's cans of food with him.

There's not much Barni can do other than repack the tramping bag and choose to accept the offering of eleven cans of dog food. He has no idea what he'll tell The Mots. Sent to buy typically delicious foodstuffs; coming home with muck for a mutt. Whatever. It'll have to do. It and whatever he tells The Mots will have to do.

"Pulls this all the time." Says The Mots. "We used to it round these parts. We used to getting less than we bargain for. Come up short in the end. Always. We give him help he gives us meat. Who he think we are?" And then, with a flash of inspiration, The Mots continues slyly "Never mind him. We pay our respects to his memory tonight. Small Gordie pushed aside by the city folk, we make moves. You follow me now. You follow me."

And all of a sudden now The Mots is moving faster than Barni's ever seen him go, it's like all the weight of his fear that the cops are everywhere is pressing down on him all at the same time, it's like the sky is infinitely heavy and the only way not to be crushed is to keep moving, to breathe heavily, to stay calm and soft, movement in excess, that's The Mots, Barni actually physically struggles to keep up, it doesn't help that The Mots is pretty much bare except the clothes on his back and Barni's got what exists of his life in tow, they're running and running and just for a sweet, harmonious second there's a pigeon landed on Barni's shoulder, looking around, Barni goes "wha-uh? You see that?" but by the time The Mots turns around to look the pigeon's gone again, off to find some other victim. So, they're running like uncaged paranoiacs away from imaginary cops and with the blessing of a totemic bird who might as well have been God.

Weirder things happen every day.

Eventually, the two of them end up outside a restaurant which has the rather simple name CHINESE FOOD. From the outside, it looks pretty much exactly as you'd imagine – images of plastic food, thick layers of dirt coat the windows (you can't even see inside), there's a bizarre community advertisement for a local psychic right next to a Missing poster for a cat named Gusgus. The Mots gives Barni a nod and barges on through the door, yells "Helen, the duck, please!" which seems to prompt a redhead behind the counter to run through the swishing plastic curtains into the kitchen. Barni still has no idea what's going on, but The Mots has sat himself down at a round table designed to seat six people, so Barni joins him there.

Looking around, Barni's impressed. This place clearly doesn't get too much traffic, it's nearly empty, and despite the name it doesn't appear to sell Chinese food at all. The outfit is classy, modern hits play through the high-rigged speakers, the tables are all large oak, it's immaculate, spotless, Barni thinks he's probably the dirtiest thing in it. And all around him, all over the walls are menu items, none of them too Chinese looking at all, most of them pretty regular, actually.

"Toast with jam" is the one that Barni's caught on, why are they selling that somewhere like this? is his first thought, but his second thought is oh man, I could really go for some toast with jam. That's not even the half of it. But The Mots seems to catch on to what Barni's thinking and barks in his characteristically unlikeable style "eh. Sit tight." That's what The Mots barks.

So Barni sits tight, trying to avoid any eye contact that's too intense with his dining partner.

He thinks about the last few days, tries to make sense of it, has to admit to himself that he has absolutely no idea what's happening. But he's going with it, and luck seems to be on his side, and he supposes that technically he's getting richer by the day. He thinks of the trade-off with Small Gordie in the gutter; two cans of legumes for eleven cans of meat-based wet dog food and begins to feel sick. Barni's worked a butchery part-time in the past and since then he hasn't been too keen to touch meat at all, has felt a little bit sick about it. He knows he should be cautious, keep the dog food, it's true, you never know when you might find yourself on a long road without a dumpster to dive in, without fortuitous food on the side of the road, and Barni still has the odd gut feeling that the day's coming, probably soon, where he'll need enough supplies to last a bit of a journey, but he can't bear the thought of dog food at all really, let alone the thought of consuming it himself, inhaling that meaty deodorant, smelling like it, not a fork in sight.

His train of thought is broken when the redhead (presumably Helen) comes out with two plates of steaming food, heaped vegetables with tiny morsels of duck meat pulled apart on top of it. The smell alone is a smell Barni can almost taste, and hell, it's been so long since he's eaten a proper meal that he digs in, barely minding that the duck is meat at all, a sudden about-face from the thinking he was just doing, thinking that would perhaps be considered ethics in the right time and place but in this time and place, in Barni's brain, was just a means to an end, registering the humiliation of a fudged trade, registering the possibility of a future, the probability, even, of an unpleasant future. Knowing that the worst stuff is yet to come and trudging on into it anyway.

So, yes, Barni eats duck meat, because he's afraid that in future he'll have to eat the ambiguous sweat that's inside those cans for dogs. He might as well savour the good stuff while he can, he reckons, and he does savour it. The Mots inhales his plate in the span of a few minutes, but Barni, well, Barni goes to town, taking his time both with and between each bite, unsure of when he'll get the chance to enjoy something like this again. When he's finally done, The Mots just gets up and leaves, which has Barni confused for a second. He approaches Helen at the front counter, wondering if he needs to organise payment God knows how, to which she leans over tits-first, says "no baby. We here at Chinese food look after you good. You best not come back here too soon. Charity only goes so far before we call for a favour. Three strikes and you're out."

Why is everybody talking in ciphers? Fuck.

Anyway, he's back out on the street now, payment mysteriously incomplete, unable to decipher where The Mots is or could have gone. He starts running, tries to retrace the path they took to get here, finds himself hopelessly lost within a turn or three, Barni's never been too great with directions, you see, and then just like that, zzzzzzzznk, there's a loud hum in the sky, it's a police helicopter, and it's descending the next block over. Barni doesn't even feel like he has a choice but to follow it, and he rounds the corner of a government building to see The Mots shoved into a straitjacket right there on the side of the road, pure terror in his eyes. They found him, they found him, these people who are no-one in particular, a mysterious force of armed arresters hiding under the guise of the name Police, one of them is quite rotund and stands with a megaphone on top of a giant trashcan, shouts "we've got you! We've got you at last! The Fordyce Killer, ladies and gentlemen! Law and order wins again!"

The policeman shouting as if he's expecting applause, but nobody's watching except for Barni. This whole display just makes Barni keel over and vomit all over the pavement in classically inelegant fashion. All that he can taste is duck meat and stomach acid.

It's at this moment that Barni realises he never learned the name of this friend (he supposes he is a friend) who's being taken away, he can't even call his name out, so instead Barni just lets out an animal cry as seven different men labelled Police lift up that mysterious vagrant, the vagrant replies with a cry of his own, they harmonise together, under the moon, their pain harmonises together, and then the helicopter's going up, away from the grid, away from the big city, toward nowhere in particular, toward somewhere people lose their selfhood altogether, The Mots will lose it all, even the little he has, his autonomy, his sense of paranoia, it'll all be gone, it'll be gone because he does know, he knows about the rest of his life, he knows he's being watched, monitored, assisted where need be, it'll be relentlessly boring, nothing to fend for, food will be given to him ready-made on a shiny plate, he'll have access to some reading material if he wants it, but none of it will be particularly interesting, he'll have access to everything he could ever need, and all at the expense of those grotesque city-dwellers, the same ones who drop dollars and cents from their pockets on the side of the road, thinking it's charity enough, thinking it's charity enough.

The Mots will be reproduced namelessly forever, a historical footnote in the Fordyce town history books. A generation or two after that, when history stops being written, he won't exist at all.

It's the next morning and Barni's going through his bag, making sure he didn't lose anything in the mayhem that was the previous night. Lighter fluid, check, half-used pen, check, suicide letter addressed to Marjorie, check, tramping bag, check, eleven cans of dog food, check, check, check, check, check, check, check, check, check, check, check. So that bag's still picking up weight, even though Barni's technically poorer than before, with both less resources and less choice. In a self-conscious moment of unease, Barni picks up and bags a large rock from the patch of dirt nearby. For what? He doesn't know, but the extra weight comforts him.

Still, he can't help the feeling he's being watched. By God? Sure, obviously, but he's also picked up The Mots' particular brand of terror, Barni can't help but feel the Police are on his tail. He knows he's an innocent, but that just makes him more paranoid. Justice is just pageantry, Barni knows this much, and he's an easy target. He has an aching headache now and a pretty heavy bag, but he pushes on for the sole reason that he doesn't want to stay in one place too long.

Sitting still, he might be found.

Sitting still, he might forget that he's meant to be finding Marjorie.

Sitting still, he won't get a step closer to her at all.

So, he moves.

In the world around Barni, lunacy persists.

The next days for Barni are marked by specific steps taken as he's hounded by the veracity of motion. He's city-hopped what would take up three grids on a map and stands outside a hotel called THE EMILE smoking a joint bummed off a fellow Samaritan when the ambulance entrance opens up and a man wearing a chef's hat and an oddly fake looking moustache bounces out the double doors, cries "compadre! Come inside, we will take care of you in here!" And, well, of course, with nothing better to do, Barni follows, an ambulance on legs or something. As they're walking and Barni's failing to get his bearings, he realises that the man in the chef's hat isn't a man at all, he's a woman, and the suspicious moustache is quite literally small black paintbrush bristles stuck onto the front of her mouth with PVC glue.

"Stop." Barni says, and the lady stops. "Am I hii-iiiiiigh?"

To which the woman just chortles, takes off the chef's hat, pulls another joint out of it like a magician, lights it up and passes it over to Barni. He doesn't turn it down, it's a free lunch, and anyway, by now the chef's taken so many corners that Barni might as well be stuck in a maze. He's a random off the street, he has no idea who she is, but hey, here they are, moving through a labyrinthine ode to pleasure, and here he is, Barni, stuck on a second waylaying odyssey, letter to Marjorie in his bag all-but-forgotten-about, and they're moving inexorably forward, forward more nobly and with more speed than Barni managed at any other stage of this process, forward, forward, toward the Hellish pit at the centre of The Emile, to the kitchen, with its fire and shine.

It's a bit later and Barni's sitting down, once again the dirtiest thing around, steaming white rice served up on top of a steaming hot white plate, glistening clean underneath it all. Nothing on top of the rice, just bland grains to sustain and sustain, while this strange chef woman goes about firing orders around her to the auxiliary kitchen employees.

"Barni." She says smirking. She pronounces his name like a venereal disease. "It is nice to meet you. I have heard much about you. My friend tells me you are lonely."

"What friend?" Barni asks in reply.

"Oh, you know. I pray every morning and I hear his voice echo clearly down from above in return. He knows exactly what you need. He knows what I need too, and I need company. It is lonely here, everybody around busy working, doing jobs, nobody to talk to. I just yell 'DISH UP' – just like that, you see," which Barni does see, as a beef mignonette is plated up through the serving window, " – and well, I need friends, it is easy to go crazy down here, no sunlight, just fire, feeling like a slave for the ancients, hmm? It is like mining but artistic. We work very hard to produce what we produce. We work very hard. We let ourselves have fun to pass the time." She rips off the faux moustache. "This, you see. I walk upstairs and pretend to be somebody else; the management barely notice. Why would they? I read Adorno; the management barely notice. Why would they? They hired me and then forgot I exist. Chefs are best left unseen, they think. Unseen, unheard, we do our job and keep them fed, keep the hotel ticking, it is not the fault of the guests that we are here, you see, they anticipate we are being paid, you see, they assume everything here is in order, everything at The Emile, but things are not in order, things are not in order here, not at The Emile. We are not paid, we take pills to keep us awake for days at a time that come in small red boxes. We cook and we cook and we cook and we throw nothing away. This hotel prides itself on being waste-free. Environmentally friendly, self-sufficient. It is a true accomplishment, really. But the human sacrifice. The human sacrifice. We know very little else. We spend our time here among fire and metal and there is not much to break up the time. So I need a friend. I sit and I pray every day, and God tells me "one must imagine Sisyphus happy," God quotes Camus, you see, well, he says that Camus stole the line from him in the first place anyway, but, well, God requotes himself through Camus' voice, and anyway, he says, one must imagine Sisyphus happy, you must imagine Sisyphus as a chef, cooking the same meals day in and day out, and the hill is people, and the rocks are pleasing them, and you are getting somewhere, and you are mattering, and you are fulfilling things. But still, it is lonely. We smoke sometimes to pass the time, so yeah, I guess you're high, we smoke sometimes to pass the time. But still, it is lonely. So I need a friend and I sit and I pray every day you are. Sitting with me, high, a friend among metal and fire. I know not much about you, Barni. I know nothing about you at all. You look like you need a shower. You look tired. The world is a tiring place, young man. The world is a very tiring place." The chef lady sits, takes off her hat, shakes it around a little, as if trying to tip something out of it, sighs, puts the hat back on again. "You are not very talkative, are you?" She says. She sighs. "Never mind." She says, she sighs. She sticks the false moustache back onto her face and puts on a manly voice.

"Never mind."

At that exact moment, a column of fire shoots up from a pan that's frying a sole fillet. A small European-looking chef with face paint designed to look like a cat shrieks, knocks the pan off the cooker. And, uh, well, uh-oh, the fish fillet's on fire and it's just come into contact with the floor, and all of a sudden there's a ring of fire around the fillet too, and it's growing, it's coming right toward Barni.

Here he is, on the road to whatever, face to face with death in the form of a small fired up fish.

The European-cat-face-paint chef continues shrieking, yelling "Fuck! Fuck! Fuck! REMI! Fuck! Fuckin'! REMI! Fuckin' DO SOMETHING! DO FUCKIN' SOMETHING! FUCK, THE FUCKIN' FIRE! THE FUCKIN' MOTH-ERFUCKIN' FISH IS ON FUCKIN' FIRE! THE FISH IS ON FUCKING, FUCKING, UH, FUCKING FIRE! Fuck!" To which this friend in the false moustache yells back "I CAN'T DO ANYTHING, KITS! I CAN'T DO ANY-THING! THE FISH IS ON FIRE! THE FISH IS ON FIRE!" That leaves one person left in the room, Barni, who at first comically tweaks his feet as if he's dancing while making a noise along the lines of "hnnnnggguuuuuuhnnnnng" and then notices the stack of dishes next to a massive, soapy sink of liquid in the corner.

This is when Barni pulls out a Winning, Athletic, Incredible Feat (a WAIF, for the well-informed). The WAIF goes like this: he slides past the flaming fish and the ring of fire, grabbing a giant metal mixing bowl on the way, keeps sliding, his right pant leg is on fire now, he throws the giant metal mixing bowl up into the air, it lands in the sink, creating a giant overflow wave, which sweeps across the floor, puts the fish out, creates a little puddle which Barni rolls around in until his pants aren't burning anymore. Once Barni's done rolling around in the remnants of his waif, Remi and Kits (presumably these are their names) break into a spontaneous round of applause, to which Barni bows like a cartoon character.

Remi does something very strange to Barni. She picks up the sopping, burnt fish off the floor and puts it on a white plate. "Bon Appetit." She says and shoves it out the serving window. "Wh-wha………?" Barni says, with that many dots before his question mark.

"Oh, you know." Remi replies "We get bad reviews quite often here anyway."

She shrugs.

"We avoid work whenever we can. We are not paid. You have helped us out. Come."

So Barni follows this bizarre woman, Remi, out of the beating, burning heart of the Emile and through another set of labyrinthine corridors to somewhere even stranger, even more claustrophobic.

Barni's waif saved the day, but Remi doesn't seem to care. She thinks to herself that she would have let the fish burn her up if it meant no more cooking. It's not true, of course, but Remi's just like everyone else.
A part of the human species, toying with violence they won't follow through on.

Barni's en suite is a literal forty-three-minute walk away from the kitchen and appears to be underground given the gradient of the corridors taken to get there. This prompts all kinds of questions, none of which Barni gets a satisfactory answer to. His concern about where on Earth he is dissipates, though, the moment he sees a pure, clean, white shower, which he steps into the moment Remi leaves with a quiet 'hullo! I mean… gudbye!," it's only Barni's second shower since the whole microwave incident. Luckily, this shower takes place without a full-blown PEC and it's only a couple of minutes before Barni finds himself dry, clean, well and truly in the nude, watching reruns of The Simpsons and thinking about the Thomas Pynchon voice cameo.

He's almost confounded by the comfort around him, doesn't know what to do with it, accidentally ends up staying up really late, enters the dawning of the next day significantly more exhausted than he otherwise may have done. Walking aimlessly around the convoluted interiors of The Emile is made even harder by the ball-and-chain of non-sleep Barni is carrying with him.

It's a solid hour or two before Barni actually manages to find another soul, but even then it's not Remi, it's not even Kits, nobody Barni recognizes, just a small hunched-over old woman stubbornly cleaning a tile that looks pretty much immaculate to Barni. He tries to get away from the woman without accidentally kickstarting a conversation he doesn't want to be a part of, but it doesn't work. The old woman spins around, exclaims, "ah, you made it! We missed you a long time ago, we missed you a long time ago, we have been waiting!" To which Barni responds with a simple and hopefully casual "mm-hmm," answered again by the lady asking "you want to help?".

Which Barni doesn't, want to help, that is, but hey, there isn't much else to do and he'll fall asleep if he isn't occupied soon, so he picks up the also-immaculate looking towel the woman is holding out and starts scrubbing the tile next to hers.

"No!" She barks. "This one! Always this one!"

So Barni scrubs all up in her personal space, too.
"You always clean the same tile?" Barni asks.

"Ae." Mutters the lady. "It's the job I am here to do."

Barni doesn't know what to say to that, so he just sits and cleans, sits and cleans, sits and cleans, for what feels like an eternity.

When he closes his eyes to rest them for just a second, he wakes up and the lady is gone. The cleaning tools have disappeared with her.

Barni's alone again, in another place he has no hold on, in a place inhabited by job-doers, but Barni doesn't even have a job.

Not one he's contracted for, anyway.

Says the person behind the counter, "you been here long?" To which Barni just gives a wry nod and says "too long." It's been seven weeks for Barni, seven weeks of being locked inside this hotel, eating shitty hotel food, locked in his room, reading books, showering three times every day for lack of a better thing to do, masturbating out of boredom most of the time if not all the time, watching You-Tube videos of academic lectures about disaster risk management; it's been seven weeks for Barni of getting enough sleep. He hasn't seen Remi in a long time, not since the day of the fire in the kitchen. One day, he's eating away at a little bit of ambiguous meat in even more ambiguous gravy when he sees a little Chef's hat popping up above the rim of his toilet. There's Remi, she's crawled up the toilet pipes, Tyrone Slothrop cum resurrection, which makes Barni question reality for all of six seconds, before Remi climbs out and lets Barni in on her plan.

"Tonight, we wait until the slugs that run this place are asleep" is what Remi says. She doesn't mean literal slugs, she means the word in its disingenuous, not-in-cor-respondence-with-reality form, "slugs" as in S.L.U.G.S., as in Small, Liberal, Ugly, Ghastly Sapiens. "And we burn the place down," Remi says.

This holds Barni up for a second, because he's kind of become comfortable with the idea of staying in just this one place, never moving forward, in fact he kind of likes that he doesn't have to try very hard, and it seems like God is inaccessible to him here, and Marjorie's a whole world away (on the outside of this labyrinth) and he doesn't have to do much at all, just lug around a bag with some random shit in it and keep on breathing, but then it clicks that he's been alone for a long time now, quite a long time, and being alone for much longer among these four walls will be not just immensely painful but potentially damage his future, and that's the moment Barni, without even asking about the specifics of the plan, just says, straight up, without warning, "yes. I'll help."

So he's rushed back to the kitchen through corridors he still barely knows how to keep track of, where Kits is waiting, outfit still complete with face paint, chopping up pieces of frozen fish and laying them across a dizzying array of kitchen utensils.

Remi speaks to Barni, the meaning at the very least is rather simple, Remi asks "you remember the first night you came here? The fire in the kitchen, the fish? We do this again, on purpose, it will look like an accident. We will help you leave, we will show you the way, and then we will come back here to burn up amongst the fishes."

Barni's a bit confused still, it seems like everything is happening really fast, like, there's not much logic to all that's going on around him and he can't quite keep his finger on the pulse of what's happening. He actually can't remember how all of this started, and, uh, he feels like he's high again, actually, though he hasn't touched any stuff in a good few weeks, few months, however long he's been here, at least not since the first night.

But he doesn't have time to sit in this sensation for too long, because all of a sudden the kitchen utensils are sitting above the gas; Kits and Remi are pouring alcohol of various types on top of it, the fire's shooting all over the show; they're knocking the utensils onto the floor; they're throwing the wooden spoons on top, the fire is rising and rising.

Among all the comedy Barni feels like he's a kid again. He's in the back seat of his mother's car.

It's raining outside and there is a bug drowning right in front of Barni's eyes, trying to cling to the car window.

He's looking out at a crematorium. He knows his father is inside but he doesn't know why. He had to leave school early on this day. He is wearing his school uniform. He wishes he could take his school uniform off. He seems so, who knows, fucking identifiable or something like that. He closes his eyes, young Barni does, and tries to sleep, but he sees images of his father, rotting, ensconced in flame, a figure caught up in the lucidity of his own destruction. Young Barni prays for a moment and then gives up in disbelief in the prospect of God. Opening his eyes, the drowning bug is gone; it managed to get away somehow; it died perhaps. Both of these things could be true. Young Barni's standing in the centre of a hotel kitchen watching some strange androgynes attempt to burn down their place of work. He's watching slices of fish, slices of white flesh burn, and he's compulsively joining in the act of adding to the fire. He's looking at the slices of burning flesh and he catches a glimpse of his father's eye for a moment, blinking at him, and Barni remembers that his father mattered and that his couch was supremely uncomfortable. One time Barni had been playing with a stray cat, he'd brought it inside. The cat had found a used syringe underneath Barni's father's couch. Barni tried to ask his father about it but didn't understand the answer. Barni tried to ask his father why he didn't live with them anymore but understood the answer too well. He's in his mother's car and they're pulling up at a hotel. He walks through endless corridors that all look the same. His father's funeral was a day ago and they're driving cross country to scatter the ashes in his father's home state. They will visit his family. These are people Barni has never met. Barni sleeps in hotel rooms that all look and feel the same and has nightmares that his father is haunting him. He gets over it a few years later, but there's a strange lady with a moustache working at a carnival on an island somewhere in his past that brings up uncomfortable memories like a feed he tries to turn off. He keeps seeing his father's face in fire. Barni writing a letter to his mother and father at school, a letter addressed Emile and Mama, a letter saying that it would be better if everything was the way everything had always been, a letter saying please. His mother burning the fish and crying and the smoke alarm going off. The cold hard feeling of rocks underneath Barni's body the night he runs away from his mother saying he wishes she'd been the one to burn instead. His mother's face transforming into a distorted drowning bug. The world through a pane of glass.

All of a sudden something out there in the world happens; Barni's brain starts collapsing in on itself. The world collapses into arrows that are all pointing (that is pressing) in on him.

The actual world itself is pressing in and Barni's body is so sore, it's been carrying so much into the rest of the world for so long. Divinely the moment of brief inspiration causes Barni to do it - something sublime starts to happen - he tips his backpack entirely upside down and everything falls out. He wakes up in the present, the contents of his upside-down-bag tossed onto the growing fire one by one, so then the lighter fluid goes first, so then the half-used pen, which in a moment of kitchened inspiration he unleashes the guts of and drinks, guzzling the ink until it's disappeared, probably poisoning himself in the process but never mind that; we poison ourselves with all sorts of things until we die. So then into the fire the skeleton of the pen sans ink, so then seven of the cans of dog food, so then Barni's about to throw the eighth can, sure, but then his body cries out to him something mad, Barni just opens the can and guzzles the dog food, glog and grog and misdemeanor, Barni's an everyman, he just hates to see food go to waste. Fuck it, so then the eighth can into the fire, this one empty. He's eaten meat for dogs, consumed ink for writing, his body is filled fiction and animal. So then that totemic stone, what the fuck is he going to do with that? Something else inside him, the fiction, maybe, tells him the rock isn't his, was never his, anyway, and he doesn't know what to do about that, so he hurls the rock toward the ceiling, which dislodges a gas-run light, which begins falling, then stays there, suspended mid-air, never falling to the ground, illuminating the scene below like a fresnel exposes the theater.

So then finally there's that letter just waiting to be burned. But that same something makes him hold onto it for a moment until he realizes he doesn't know even where he is or what is happening to him, he just catches a glimpse of a security camera in the ceiling high above him, somebody watching(!?) but then it clicks and the camera is just the hovering gas-light, and it falls back to earth, hits Barni square between the eyes, knocking him to the ground, man in pain next to burning pile….so then Barni's crawling with letter in hand, and he can't quite describe what it is, what it is that makes him do it, but he plunges his hand deep into the fire and watches the letter addressed to Marjorie go up in smoke, it's ash and burning and horror and deep orange, and there it is, he's come here for what? for no reason? to destroy? to resurrect? and so the letter's all burned up and gone, it might as well never have existed, but, wait, Barni's hand is in the god damn fire too, what insanity, why did he do that?, so he pulls his hand out, looks at it, waxy and mid-destruction, lets out a scream, passes out, fire raging so around that it may as well be part of him.

Here's Barni, rest of the world behind him, about to be burned up because

all it took to ignite was a letter.

6

Like a Phoenician there's a moment where Barni seems to recognise a system to the chaos, until of course he realizes he must be hallucinating because the system is a woman, phoenix-like, apparently burning too. He feels himself moving, floating, as if of somebody else's accord. Barni sees a birds-eye view of his own body dragged from the kitchen of the Emile, almost laughs for a moment to think that this might as well make him God, looking at the world from the pigeons' eye, before he passes out, unaware of his own body no more.

Here she is. Emerging toward the fire, the woman that has been waited for. The woman that has been chased. She walks like a lonely swallow. Her skin is chameleonic. She resembles the road; the road is paving itself over as she propels, propels herself forward. Carrying with her the weight of all of her history, and her country's history, and Barni, she pulls her shawl over her shoulders. She's much older than anybody might think just looking at her.

She resembles the road; the road is paving itself over as she, chameleonic, arrives. She waits to pave her face with her pathway. She in processual destruction, she of the road, she of the night time, she who's been hurt, she without child. She as she, she as signifier, she signifies the road, she is now the road, moving upon it she might as well be it, run over, weighed down by figures resembling people. She, transformed into being by the words of others, she, reality collapsing, she, the end-game, the final boss, the last obstacle for Barni to cross, the last of the l ast. She who has no need for style arrives with style in tow.

A light tingling in her palm tips off her eyes to stay open. Her eyelashes bigger than her eyes. She resembles the creator. Droopy hoods, worn- out clothing, dismissive manner, and more, and more. The walking figure of grief; succubus; whippoorwill; ghost; nothing left, vacancy, a pigeon on legs.

Her feet are bare and dirty, as if they already picked up the lint and detritus dropped by earlier travelers. There is no telling why she is so late. There is no telling how she came to be here. Call it 'fate,' call it 'randomness,' call it 'coincidence,' call it 'serendipity,' call it 'writing,' call it 'deus ex machina,' call it 'whatever you will,' call it by what it is, she's here, she is here and came to be here by arriving. On these occasions, merely to arrive is enough. To make an appearance is close to surviving. "Keeping on keeping on," KOKO, as they say, a double knock-out phrase, meaningless and hopeful, something like that anyway[1]. She has done enough, she has arrived.

She has arrived on the scene of a fire at the exact moment that a bizarre, short, fragile looking man is screaming, skin on his hand melting, in absolute disarray. Barefoot and all she starts running toward him (some sense of basic human decency and a modicum of politeness encourage her to, oh, I don't know, save this guy, or something), and then she watches him collapse, watches his spinal column give way into the intense caress of the fire.

For just a moment, it seems like the man's spirit (green, waxy, sick-looking) exits his body. She pauses. But then she's back in it, adrenal glands pumping. She manages to get a hold of the man's shoe, accidentally pulls it off, grabs the man's foot instead, drags him away from the fire, kitchen, hotel, onto that negligible and mostly passable road.

---

[1] And today in the newspaper: in ML, Sd.: a man described as a possi- ble "InCel" (Involuntary Celibate) accidentally blew his hand off while tinkering with a bomb that authorities believe was meant to kill women, according to an affidavit.

He's in the arms of the woman he's been waiting for and just like that Barni wakes up, looks at her, actually doesn't see her for a moment, she's that chameleonic, or he's that incoherent, one of the two, "are you a ghost," "no baby, just calm yourself down a while, rest, you in pain," and he passes back out, but asleep this time, right there in her arms, middle of the trafficless road, two people connecting over – what? – nothing? – their shared livingness? – their shared experience with fire and pavement? – something like it, so, yes, here they are, Barni – a survivor, you could say, a victim of God – and this lady, blonde, road-like, blending in, historic, almost, and you'd be right, you'd be right, phoenix, she falls asleep next to him in the middle of the road, and you'd be right, you'd be right, their bodies fight together just as if they were meant to, and you'd be right, you'd be right, her name is Marjorie, her name is Marjorie and she's here with Barni.

Barni, then, and Marjorie, no worries about the rest of the world, no worries at all.

7

BARNI (laughing): There was. A letter. It um it said sorry and I think he wrote it he's dead.

MARJORIE: What? Who? Sit yourself down. Drink this.
(Handing him water).

BARNI: I saw something, I, there was a letter, I found it. I found this letter and I think whoever wrote it is dead. Something about Sisyphus. Getting too close to you. Everything you said being true.

MARJORIE (silently): Mm. I was wondering when I'd finally hear about this.

BARNI (sinking): I don't think I can tell you anything else.

MARJORIE: That's okay, dear. You've been through enough, by the looks of you.

BARNI: I was meant to be in a hotel in Mexico right now. How's that? How's that? They kicked me out.

MARJORIE: Honey, you're going to have to talk a whole lot clearer than that if you want me to get what you're saying.

BARNI: I started where I always start. And then things keep on happening. I met this guy, he, he got arrested. I don't really understand what for, even though I know somewhere deep inside me. And I keep seeing things. Things keep on happening. They told me I was crazy, before I came here, I mean. I was hearing things and they felt right somehow and I (clutching sand) wanted to go where they told me and how. I don't know what else I could have done. And I listened to the voices – it, uh, it was a bird, a pigeon, or maybe lots of them – and they took me there, to this place, some, farm, something like that, nobody was there, and there was this letter, it had this name, Marjorie, on it, and I thought I had to bring it to you, and I spent so long thinking about finding you but not doing anything about it. I'm a fraud, I feel like I'm walking through somebody else's world. And then you came here, I was so hot and you came here. I didn't even find you, this just happened. Things keep just happening to me and I don't know what to do about that. I get lost a little bit sometimes inside myself. I keep trying to keep trying but it doesn't work like that. I lose things that don't seem like they matter (dropping sand) and they do matter, they do. When my dad died I took the batteries from his watch and put them into this shitty little remote controlled car that I used to play with all the time. I ended up driving that thing into a fucking swamp. The batteries are, I think, still there, just, congealing.

MARJORIE: I am listening to you, you know.

BARNI: What do you mean by that?

MARJORIE: I can hear that you are saying words. I am listening to the words. I am interpreting and responding to them in kind.

BARNI: That's a very weird thing to say, uh, miss.

MARJORIE: Barni, now, come on. You're a good reader. You should know about this interpretive business.

BARNI: What do you mean?

MARJORIE (taking off her face): Really Barni, you should have suspected something like this.

BARNI (looking forlornly away, not noticing just yet): The counterfeit and the imaginary are one and the same. Whatever you want I can't give it –

MARJORIE (bird): You didn't do your job, Barni. You took too long. You got distracted. All you needed to do was fucking….find me. Find her, I guess. I'm disappointed in you, Barni. This didn't need to be so complex. You made this ridiculous. You transformed the cartography of your life into something like a cartoon. What the fuck, man? (Shrinking down to pigeon-size). I am trying to get at something very simple, you know. I am trying to get at something very simple.

(Barni raises his foot and brings it down on Marjorie – no, the pigeon's – head, over and over again, until her head is flattened, a shadow of a shadow of God, a red shadow on yellow-streaked pavement, the rest of her body full and plump, pregnant, even, full of possibility, but snapped, it detaches from the top of her, no top-down divination here, God is dead, or at least this one pigeon is, and Barni does it, yelling and shrieking; a yellow car slows down to watch and then drives off. Two days later she's a remarkable bit of roadkill. Looks almost like a stone.)

PART

TWO

"the Prophet then urinates on the „des-ert"

–Thomas Pynchon

looks around him / doesn't recognise anything /
objects don't seem to be objects anymore / there
is a faint incoherent haze around everything

the world is inchoate / foreign / Barni touches
his own head but his hand does not feel anything
/ not anything physical / his brain collapses in on
itself / there's a road in front of him

it looks like a road at least / but it isn't solid /
there isn't anything distinct / about it / not that
Barni knows for sure anyway

the clouds open up above / it starts / to rain /
three birds fly overhead / wing / wing it / the
world is a perfect image / the world is a perfect
image of itself

itself is nothing to speak of /
attempting some sort of transformation /
I am nothing short of short / Barni thinks to his
self / himself

in a flurry / the wings of the world surround him
/ if he can think of himself like that / at this time
/ he's losing his grip / yes / he is losing his grip
on the world /
in a moment he is inside the belly of something
/ much bigger than him / he thinks / Geppetto
in the whale / he thinks / I am Ahab's leg / he
thinks / I have found myself inside of a giant
peach / he thinks / the world is me / so much
more than me / he thinks / I am a bar of soap
with a voice in a play set in Dublin / he thinks / I
am Malone Molloy Unnamed in a Pit / he thinks
/ I am inside the belly of something / it is much
bigger than I / at that moment / a sudden echoing / a booming / something monolithic

it is speaking /
rumbling

before / not here / precisely / but on some similar inchoate journey / we have given you instruc-
tions / this / us / the avian watchers / we have
seen you burn information up / we have seen you
diminish story / we have seen you act your lonely
self upon the world / we have seen you commit
yourself to our death /
you are capable /
of destroying us /
therefore we must destroy you first / look around
you / you are inside a belly / a giant / stomach
/ it will fill with acid / when I stop speaking to
you / it will fill with acid / you will dissolve / no
longer in a body / you will be scattered across the
road below / you / what you are conscious of
wh / what / uh / hng? / ha / of / wh / what
says Barni /
God replies /
I am / you know / God / we've met before / you
fucking killed me / you killed me so I brought
you here / so I could watch you dissolve / inside
my self / so I could dissolve / scatter / you
yeah / the road below / you'll have some new
cans / you'll have the same lighter / the same
lighter fluid / nothing else / not even hands /
nothing to carry them with / nothing to offload
them with / they'll just be there
everything you ever were / will be with you /
with nothing / you can do about it / this is Heav-
en / where all the fucking
Christians / wish they'd be allowed into / it ain't
so good here after all / I'm tired / still / I am
merely trying to / huh / uh / help you out

then the voice is gone / Barni wonders how he
understands it / actually / like for real / since
when could I understand pigeons / now that I
think of it / I don't remember ever not / understanding them / I only remember being here / in
the now / there is nothing behind me / invisibil-
ity ahead of me /

it eats away at him / his leg erodes into bone /
Barni's nothing physical / he's a pathetic / worn
down husk of words / imagined / literally not
real / a figure in disappearance / his mouth is
being swallowed up by this much larger mouth /
it is not romance / it is not eros

it is mere / violence / in Heaven

his flesh is no longer / flesh he thinks about /
Scarlett Johansson / his spirit hovers above a
pool of filth and pith / his spirit hovers above
his flesh

watches a sparrow fly down from above / wait
what? / yeah fly down from above / aren't we
inside a bird already? / fly down from above /
begin to drink the acid / to guzzle Barni's physical self

Barni watches the bird shit him back out again /
he's turned from antihero into literal shit / but
he's still here / somehow / disembodied / watching

he fills a strange weight in his heart / reaches out
to touch it with what would have been his hands
/ it's a can of dog food / motherfucker / but his
hand just goes right on through / his hand is an
illusion

he isn't a thing anymore / he's not an

ontological being

he's a / theory

he's a / man in a foreign landscape

he's a / man surpassing his self into Heaven

he's a / memory of somebody who just got eaten
inside the stomach of something avian

he's a / lonesome cowboy with a long way to go

he's a / Sisyphus for the afterlife

he'll repeat things / the same journey again / over / along a different road / this is what he's stuck with now / just some replicated version of selfhood

/ this replica narrative
/ he knows it could be worse
/ in fact he knows what he has to do this time the rest of the world shrinks back away from him / as it shrinks / away from that which overarches / he recedes back into himself / invisibly / he hovers to the side of the road / it's bizarrely concrete

[and Byzantine]

for Heaven / not really what you would expect / and now Barni is walking / but he doesn't have feet / he can still somehow feel contact between the paved grey under foot and his soul / but he doesn't have nerve endings / his body receded in on his spirit / so Barni is walking

forward / and forward
and / forward

not knowing where he's headed / like a battery in a circuit / coming back for Marjorie? / coming back for something else / his path has been set not once now / but twice now / by the same fucking thing / the same hieroglyph / sycophant / narcissist / creator / dictator

/ his father being planted in the ground

/ nothing growing

/ an insect on the windshield

fronted with the front end of our lives / in a vortex / swirling

and this turns everything back in on itself / "we" transforms / back into "Barni" / yes / Jenny's teeth flicker in the sunlight / she says "aw, shucks, Barni, but" / and he's twelve again / he splices his hand between his leg and feels a small patch of wet / she says "creep" / she says / nothing else after that / she says / she wants to get close to someone who's willing to listen to her / she says / nothing else after that / she plays basketball with the other guys / they all resemble each other / she becomes a punk rocker / she tries heroin / she ends up working as an administrator for a finance company / she tries heroin again / she quits her job / she becomes a creep / the rest of the world is out there / she transcends where she starts / the words no longer hold her in / we keep trying to limit these / people / these people / limited to their role / Barni is no longer the centre / it all falls apart / the spine cracks

the spine

cracks

in the dream / the spine is a catastrophe statue

mounted / rising high toward the clouds / their own monument / the sky's monument / the statuary recedes into identity making / boredom / there is nothing much special about it / it looks like every man who has ever lived / Barni's father too / the every man and every / man made creature / the cycle moves somewhat along these lines / if it is a cycle / if it repeats / moves in and around /

his father being planted in the ground

/ I want you to drink your milk I want you to drink your milk

/ an ant crawling over the shovel

/ somebody laughing and stifling that with a cough

/ nothing more and nothing less than /

his father being planted in the ground

like an insect / netted with dirt and mulch / netted in false prospect / failed / veiled / by the actual literal ground / on what grounds / on what we become

a white lady / all tits and no eyes / leans over a bowl of noodles and whispers from the inside of Barni's brain / we eat / consume / consume with me Barni / in this brief moment Barni is both on the ground and not on the ground / Barni exists 'elsewhere' as well as / here / wherever whatever / there is some correlative distance between this fiction and that reality / Barni serving looks / looking good / Barni flirting with this lady / with his eyes / the room in Barni's pants getting smaller / what a silly way to think / he recognizes her from somewhere / your brain needs to do too much / processual / he is processual in his existence / why this woman is so important to him / Barni cannot really tell / he's not even a physical being / how he has this sensation in his lower half? / he couldn't tell you / he couldn't tell you a thing
he's wrapped in rapt attention at what / unfolds

/ life distinct around him like disarray

/ disarray distinct around him like origami

/ a swan

/ there is something visual happening here in
Barni's subconscious / but he can't see / hear /
it / there is something / uh / unusual / going on
/ there are places to be / but there is no Barni
to inhabit those places / no Barni that exists beyond this / uh / field of linguistic construction
/ anyway / what's that / that he's saying / he's
saying / who / who are you / am I / questioning
/ really / not / saying / what a / disaster / what
a / ceaseless journey

he thinks / foucault / he thinks / jesus christ /
he thinks / foucault / he thinks / fuck you / he
recalls a verse from the bible / never mind / not
quite / he's hungry / he's hungry / he wishes
he still had a voice / something to shout with /
something to be able to speak with

Barni's tone has been taken from him / raped by
the great invisible hand of God / I did not consent to living like this / Barni thinks / I did not
consent to living / like this / Barni's consciousness becomes aware of something else for a moment / between the divine and the temporal /
a blonde woman boiling potatoes / is that her?
Jeanne Dielman / no / Barni thinks he recognis-
es her / but only for a second / and then he's
moving on / next to a bird / retentive / attentive
when

out of no place / the police arrive / the police
with their megaphones / big words / horrors

/ Barni mutters / but one of them stands out
/ one in their uniform / what happened to the
lyric? / wasn't this a poem? / wasn't this meant
to be beautiful? / but instead the policeman yells
/ hands up / seriously hands up / an instruction
Barni tries to follow / but can't / you know /
what with the fact he has no hands / and all /
and all that stuff / stuff like that / so Barni tries
to yell back / I can't / I can't do it / my hands
won't do what you want them to do / so the
policeman fires a shot

straight through without doing anything / the
policeman looks frightened for a second / it's as
if consequence is right around the corner / but
then consequence disappears / the corner disappears too / the policeman is here / where he has
always been / doing his job

/ somehow Barni senses forward momentum

even though there is nothing ahead / and nothing behind

the road is tactile

liceman / out of / reach / reaching beyond and
further / than this / whatever / this / is

the lady / u know the one / she kept cleaning
those tiles / no / that one tile / inside Emile /
the Emile that is / the place / not the name /
the name as attenuated to place / swamp-like
furore and the noise of a red light ticking on
and then off / a clown? / a broiled face? / a
recurring image of a swamp with a faded vehicle
inside it / the closing shot of Psycho / but the
one everybody forgets about / we kept cleaning
as we reached around inside Emile / hm? / yes
for a brief moment the sky opens up / reflects
the flattening plane of all that shit that's going
on / going on underneath / retention is difficult
for Barni for a moment / ongoing / he doesn't
know where his body begins and where it begins
to disappear / and then his spirit's wasted / on
the side of the road
after a minor cataclysmic interaction with some
/ thing / it resembles a pigeon / or at least a
caricature / he finds himself

some approximation of his self / at least / spat
out / on the road side

get on living / he tells this other-he / get on living man / he feels like he might be transforming
into something he's not /
on trial

/ the more you worry / about the big G / God
/ the less you'll accomplish / at least from here
on out / all this it happened / to prove something to you / don't you know that? / don't you
know that? / I am trying to get at something
very simple
/ I am trying to get at something very simple /
my body / I embody my runes
I know first what's left to do /
and where is left to be.

ground sans lofty ambitions / the rest of what comes next isn't for him anymore / certainly not / it's for the people he's leaving behind / the talons and the wife / the other nucleus he'd lived next to for so long before the hole in the / real world / window / whatever / curtains up on Marjorie / raised from vulnerable terror to something new now something / post grief post /

everything / sans the world / a true materialist sensation
she looks at the patterns on the ceiling / un-necessary / remnants of the twentieth century post-war reconstruction architectural style / how does she know that? / she doesn't / she looks at the patterns on the ceiling / anyway

~~~ -- - - -- ~~~ --- ~~~ ----- ~~~~~ ~ ~.
---- ~ ,. . . ~~~-----`~~''~~-- - - - -- - ~ ``
`~````~~~~

~~~ -- - - -- ~~~ --- ~~~ ----- ~~~~~ ~ ~.
---- ~ ,. . . ~~~-----`~~''~~-- - - - -- - ~ ``
`~````~~~~

~~~ -- - - -- ~~~ --- ~~~ ----- ~~~~~ ~ ~.
---- ~ ,. . . ~~~-----`~~''~~-- - - - -- - ~ ``
`~````~~~~

~~~ -- - - -- ~~~ --- ~~~ ----- ~~~~~ ~ ~.
---- ~ ,. . . ~~~-----`~~''~~-- - - - -- - ~ ``
`~````~~~~

~~~ -- - - -- ~~~ --- ~~~ ----- ~~~~~ ~ ~.
---- ~ ,. . . ~~~-----`~~''~~-- - - - -- - ~ ``
`~````~~~~

~~~ -- - - -- ~~~ --- ~~~ ----- ~~~~~ ~ ~.
---- ~ ,. . . ~~~-----`~~''~~-- - - - -- - ~ ``
`~````~~~~

~~~ -- - - -- ~~~ --- ~~~ ----- ~~~~~ ~ ~.
---- ~ ,. . . ~~~-----`~~''~~-- - - - -- - ~ ``
`~````~~~~

~~~ -- - - -- ~~~ --- ~~~ ----- ~~~~~ ~ ~.
---- ~ ,. . . ~~~-----`~~''~~-- - - - -- - ~ ``
`~````~~~~

hovering out of reach of her own perception of
what is and is not / materialism / object ontolo-
gies / she's a realist /
firmly in the here and now / both a yes man
and a she /
man / a perpetual rejectionist of sorts / dating
an ex projectionist of sorts / though no more /
she supposes / she still makes these silly jokes /
inside her / head / at least /

the odd thing to laugh at / it's healthy / enough
for some

the jokes continue / to abound / to replenish
her / from the inside /
for the most part her life is /
what?
/ forgotten?
/ forgettable?

/ something else / the television news plays
images of bombings and terror / something is
happening in the Congo / something is happening in Kabul / she doesn't bother to make the
effort / to understand
/ images of a lot of skin that doesn't look like
Marjorie's / it's foreign / cinematic almost /
she shouldn't think this way / she does think
this way / she's a woman of her time you might
suppose / wait / a woman of this time / we all
know the type
/ we keep creating things / out of no things /
why fear God / he's not even there / most likely
/
about and around / whatever they say / dragged
to church on Sunday mornings / thinking in
forms and shapeshifts / taxonomies / there's
something beyond the sugar bowl
/ there must be something beyond this / or
that / sugar bowl / there must be some / thing
that will tell me what you are / where you are
/ have gone / why / so forth / all that / Barni
/ come the fuck on / she thinks / she even
says aloud / you can't just write that / that's /
you've fucked / leave that there / say sorry and
then die / that's it / we thought you were over
/ everything / all this / fucked up / stuff / it's
fucked is it that / is that it? / is it that / because
/ is it /

becoming friends again / you've / fuck / you
and I
/ thought you knew what you were doing / you
told me you were seeing a shrink / you told us /
you told / us / you've fucked it / Barni / Barni
/ Barni / everything, all of / it / what? / is that
it / is it that/ that's easier than listening to me /
I wouldn't have accepted your apology anyway /
if you'd said it / to me / i mean / not on paper
/ i mean if you'd done it somewhere or somehow else / what? / ha /

i can't laugh at this /

she's crying now

/ tears spill over the kitchen sink

domestic goddess / yeah

something like that / alone on a Saturday /
bleach / chaste icon
stories of his mother / rolling her r's and serving bland / rice pudding

/ telling the story / his r's roll too / pudding /
not spiced at all / and in transparent bowls /
kind of exciting / ! / because of that / the abil-
ity to see straight through the receptacle / the
vehicle / the artistry of the single mother

not by choice she supposes / at the end of the
day the artistry probably wasn't / a choice

the most beautiful accidents occur / in the
kitchen
the most beautiful accidents occur / on the
streets
the most criminal institution / is a preventative
measure
akin to / tape / roller wire / kinship / all of that
and more

sink toward the drain / shit / appeal / to God
for help / moving / forward but not forward
/ at the same time / leaning / tipping over /
a little tea pot / short and stout / tip me over
and pour me out / ! / a laugh / a little laugh /
silence / same as always

/ an insect scuttling abdominally / across the
ceiling

decorative decrepitude / pretend / pretend /
pretence / she looks for a moment over at the
Lucy Ellmann book / over on that shelf / the
big oak one / and smiles / a moment of comfort and warmth amid the rest of it all /

this is another place / a place within a place / a
place within whatever is / set up / the theatre
of the visible / the invisible registrar / ? /

she all of a sudden knows that this must be
the rest of her /
life / like this / the rest of her life in the kitchen
/ hovering above the sink / restricted to an
image of what was / what could be
/ what will be /
inside her / never mind the rest / a knock at
the door / a cute young man with a box of
doughnuts / his face resembles her ex lover /
the one that was buried / cremated / both of
them / shot into space /

memorialised in words
/ like the best of us
/ and the worst
/ history is catching up with her

/ on the radio Melvyn Bragg talks about the
Roman Empire / it's with an accent / she never
wants to hear that voice again / not ever / the
batteries in the bin / on the floor / taken out /
the radio is a cavity / a dental surgery / awry /
gone wrong / the sound of the tap drip
/ dripping / scary / unlike anything else / unlike
a recognition / what's the sense being made of
this thing / what's that? / that's what / the Bible

wrong direction / hm? / it spills over beyond
itself
/ like an egg / a dripping yolk / a yellow mess /
not like at all / just an egg / an actual egg / a
lady / a hen / a bird / a / what? /

/ too much weight
/ lose some weight
/ get a new dress / a new dress? / i don't need
/ anything / anything like that / anyway / what
would i wear it for? / where would i / i? / wear
something like that / ! / ha / too bad / what a
joke / a good laugh / very practical, though /
very / nnnngk / what's the word / swish / very
/ debutante / yes / a prima donna / yes / a
memory of Italy
/ a glimmer of better times
/ the sunny day
/ that sunny day / in Italy / we kissed each other / Barni and I kissed each other / we kissed /
ate food / touched each other / with our eyes /
we kissed each other / in the sun / in Italy /

/ and we did it too / which our parents didn't
want /

we did it next to the morgue

PART

THREE

"For every creature, death is the unique moment par excel-lence. The qualitative time of life is retroactively defined in relation to it. It marks the frontier between the duration of consciousness and the objec-tive time of things. Death is nothing but one moment after the other, but it is the last. Doubtless no moment is like any other, but they can neverthe-less be as similar as leaves on a tree, which is why their cinematic repetition is more paradoxical in theory than in practice."
-André Bazin

○

Marjorie is outside of the perpetual workings of temporal and eternal nature.

Her bookshelf is populous. Often, she likes to take down a heavy tome, thumb it, and place it back on the shelf. It helps her recall herself to who she used to be, and who she used to be around. He had read a lot, and difficult books, and often, and she had often engaged them too, but more flirtatiously. And then he was gone, the words seeming too these days to be perpetual escapees. The spilled egg yolk gesticulates away from her across the tiles. The dust is unsettled.

That is all.

The quiet exists and abounds.

Marjorie steps toward the sink. She pulls out from underneath a small cubic blue washcloth. She scrubs the mess underneath her. Albeit slowly it comes up. She rinses the cloth. Goes back to the mess. Rinses the cloth. Goes back to the mess. Rinses the cloth for a final time. Moves away from the sink. Wipes her left hand on her apron. There's still a wedding ring encircling one of her fingers. Two other rings also.

She raises the needle on the turntable. Places down a record. Liszt; Faust Symphony. Diminishes the needle. The music roars and silences in alternating fashion. It mimics Marjorie's application to the egg yolk. She sways from side to side. She thinks of him. A photo above the mantelpiece. A funerary hand-out. Gone too soon. A smiling photo. There's a halo of sunlight resting just above it.

Marjorie's swaying in time with the gentle trees outside.

There is a subtle rapping noise on the door. It tapers off brilliantly and transforms into the chiming of a bell. Marjorie halts mid-movement. She takes seven steps, each one resembling its own sin, and throws the door open wide. The boy behind it is pretty like a girl. He has a box in one hand and a phone in the other.

"This is for you" he says.

"Oh." Marjorie replies. "I didn't order anything."

"Delivery address said it was here, ma'am. No name on the order."

"Nobody else lives here."

"It's yours, then."

"What is it?"

"I'm from a bakery down the road, ma'am. Doughboys. We opened just last week."

"I didn't know that."

"Well, you know. Business is picking up around here again. You know, after…"

"Yes."

"Well, you have a good day."

"You too."

They stare at each other for a moment, hanging onto some glimpse of alterity. Both are exonerated from themselves.

"Oh," says Marjorie. She takes the box.

And then it's back to the quietude and solace.

There are six donuts in the box. Mango cream; salted caramel pretzel; Japanese bean curd; cinnamon; cherry and vanilla; bacon and maple syrup. Takes her time to eat them all. There is only her. Some have gone stale by the time she reaches them.

At another time, when they're all gone, she opens the front door and places the empty box back outside. Some stray dog will pick it up. Or some stray something.

The kitchen counter is sculpted in direct relationship to dust. It has gathered here over time, now that it has been allowed to. Congregations of particles that are unrelated to each other beyond their commensality dance in each other's orbits. These minor constellations respond to the infinite abyss of the tile bench below. Traffic abounds; earlier in the day, shards of sunlight would splinter through shadows now in hiding.

Echoing images camouflage themselves among the milieu. A blender is switched off and unplugged. Just above it, the power switch has been left turned on. The odd speck of dust on occasion will insert itself into the holes, disrupting the intricate balance of this order. Elsewhere, the tap drips lazy water every few seconds. The fireplace is incommensurably empty. Two of the light fixtures reject their ineptitude, accept faulty bulbs anyway. The wiring here sparks infrequently now. All natural or nothing. Lights are dismissed. They are infrequently employed these days. When they are, it is a sudden and beautiful wake-up call.

The window on the Eastern side of the building frames an overhung oak tree. In the dimness of the night, it at times evokes the distant memory of an olden-time horror film, the kind that no longer gets made, not in the same ways, anyhow.

The stairs are dusted with specks, a none-too significant materialisation of passage. The roof houses more moths than one would expect. The beams curve Westward, toward the room Marjorie sleeps in. The air is anaesthetic.

Resisting the urge to sleep Marjorie picks up a half-finished book. Camus. The Myth of Sisyphus. She opens the spine from where the spine is now permanently folded. She attempts to take in the words.

The groping, anxious quest of a Proust, his meticulous collecting of flowers, of wallpapers, and of anxieties, signifies nothing else. At the same time, it has no more significance than the continual and imperceptible creation in which the actor, the conqueror, and all absurd men indulge every day of their lives. All try their hands at miming, at repeating, and at recreating the reality that is theirs. We always end up by having the appearance of our truths. All existence for a man turned away from the eternal is but a vast mime under the mask of the absurd. Creation is the great mime.

The meaning barely registers. Her eyes are heavy, after all of this, but the rest of her feels lighter, as if there's air underneath her wings that wasn't there before, like her body is filled with free, coursing energy, like a silhouette; it ricochets and resembles happiness, the happiness she felt before it all, before he died, before he was buried, before her sentences became so terse and miserable - before hyphens disappeared, before she forgot how to use a semicolon; there was a time when Marjorie was a writer and had much to say, there was a time she was like a silhouette, a God, before the rest of this, before the emergence of what came next, there was a time she performed a version of herself on paper; the world had a different hue then, a different shape, she went for many walks, she was poor, she was a mountaineer, she had strong arms, she knew a lot about a lot of things; she forgot it all after a while, started cleaning the house, became a silhouette of somebody else, a toxic representation of things she was not and will never be, a representation of the real, a misconception, a want, a desire, a dame to be rescued, a silhouette, somebody engaging with the immaterial real, a silhouette, a ghost, a minor player in somebody else's story, a silhouette, a goal, part of a bigger design, a deus ex machina, a chemical configuration of ideas, a silhouette, a woman, a void, a woman, silhouette.

From somewhere else beyond the page the meaning spills more than transfers into her. Even so she finally comes to an understanding at the crucial moment. One must imagine Sisyphus happy. Things will continue.

There is the final period. Then there is the blank page that comes after.

Marjorie picks up an origami crane from Barni's side of the bed and places it inside the book. It signifies something.

She closes the pages on the bird.

Josiah Morgan was born in Christchurch, New Zealand, in 2001.
He is a disability support worker by day, and a performer by night. His other books include Inside the Castle (2019, Amphetamine Sulphate), The Texas Chainsaw Massacre (2022, Amphetamine Sulphate) and Circles (2020, Selffuck). He's had a talk with Jesus.

Josiah Morgan would like to sincerely thank
Matthew Lang
Ben Herriot
Emma Reynolds
Samuel M. Moss
Nathan Dragon
Steven Arcieri
and Evan Femino for the kindness to collaborate

The road continues.
Barni walks with it...

Published by Feral Dove
Books

ISBN 979-8-9856764-1-9

Thank you for being here

Book design by Evan Femino

feraldove.com

CPSIA information can be obtained
at www.ICGtesting.com
Printed in the USA
BVHW042000010522
635577BV00009B/194

9 798985 676419